PRAISE FOR

GOOSEBERRY PARK
AND THE MASTER PLAN

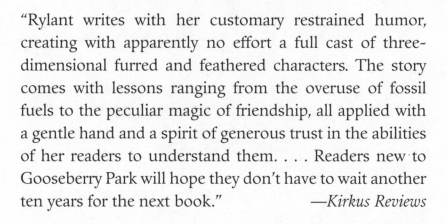

"Rylant writes with her customary restrained humor, creating with apparently no effort a full cast of three-dimensional furred and feathered characters. The story comes with lessons ranging from the overuse of fossil fuels to the peculiar magic of friendship, all applied with a gentle hand and a spirit of generous trust in the abilities of her readers to understand them. . . . Readers new to Gooseberry Park will hope they don't have to wait another ten years for the next book." —*Kirkus Reviews*

★ "Howard's black-and-white illustrations build on the story's ample humor (as when he shows a blissed-out Murray enjoying a Reiki session from Gwendolyn the hermit crab) while Rylant unspools a quietly magical tale of cooperation and kindness, with a gentle environmental undercurrent." —*Publishers Weekly*, starred review

"A sweet tale of friendship and teamwork." —*Booklist*

★ "This contemporary tale is a surefire winner. Rylant's inspired writing gives readers a humane understanding of drought and its consequences. The importance of family and friendship is reinforced as every creature rises to the occasion. The characters are wonderfully defined. The cartoonish black-and-white drawings add to the fun. Vocabulary is sophisticated. . . . Rylant does it again with this wonderful tale of nature, friendship, and family; a must-have." —*School Library Journal*, starred review

ALSO BY CYNTHIA RYLANT

Gooseberry Park

GOOSEBERRY PARK
AND THE MASTER PLAN

CYNTHIA RYLANT ❧ ARTHUR HOWARD

Beach Lane Books New York London Toronto Sydney New Delhi

BEACH LANE BOOKS

An imprint of Simon & Schuster Children's Publishing Division

1230 Avenue of the Americas, New York, New York 10020

BEACH LANE BOOKS is a trademark of Simon & Schuster, Inc.

For information about special discounts for bulk purchases, please contact Simon & Schuster Special Sales at 1-866-506-1949 or business@simonandschuster.com.

The Simon & Schuster Speakers Bureau can bring authors to your live event. For more information or to book an event, contact the Simon & Schuster Speakers Bureau at 1-866-248-3049 or visit our website at www.simonspeakers.com.

Also available in a Beach Lane Books hardcover edition.

Book design by Sonia Chaghatzbanian

The text for this book is set in Guardi LT Std.

The illustrations for this book are rendered in pencil, India ink, and wash.

Manufactured in the United States of America

0417 FFG

First Beach Lane Books paperback edition March 2016

10 9 8 7 6 5 4 3 2

The Library of Congress has cataloged the hardcover edition as follows:

Rylant, Cynthia.

Gooseberry Park and the Master Plan / Cynthia Rylant ; illustrated by Arthur Howard.

p. cm.

Summary: Stumpy, Murray, Gwendolyn, and Kona recruit Herman the crow and 200 owls to help with their Master Plan to assist the animals of Gooseberry Park that are in trouble because of a months-long drought.

ISBN 978-1-4814-0449-5 (hardcover)

ISBN 978-1-4814-0451-8 (eBook)

[1. Droughts—Fiction. 2. Animals—Fiction. 3. Cooperativeness—Fiction.]

I. Howard, Arthur, illustrator. II. Title.

PZ7.R982Gp 2015

[Fic]—dc23

2013046528

ISBN 978-1-4814-0450-1 (pbk)

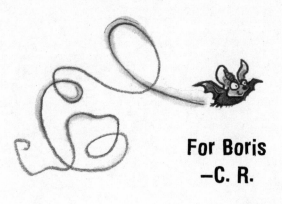

For Boris
—C. R.

For Beverly
—A. H.

Contents

1. Fine Friends 1

2. Rain Matters 8

3. Kona's Conviction 15

4. A Genius 24

5. Up All Night 33

6. Morton 40

7. Only One Owl 49

8. The Master Plan 54

9. Decoys 67

10. Nerves 74

11. If You Can Dream It . . . 82

12. . . . You Can Do It 93

13. Perfectly 98

14. Home 104

GOOSEBERRY PARK

AND THE MASTER PLAN

1

Fine Friends

It is not an easy job raising three children, especially if those children seem always to be hanging upside down in a tree.

Such was the life of Stumpy Squirrel, the busiest squirrel mother in all of Gooseberry Park.

It was all Murray's fault, of course. Bats most naturally hang upside down and are good at it. Murray was a bit of a show-off anyway, so he swung by his toes whenever anyone passing by happened to look up.

Murray was Stumpy's tree mate, best friend, and self-appointed uncle to her three children: Sparrow, Top, and Bottom. And he could be a very naughty influence, as when he taught the children to hang by their toes, and they drew all sorts of remarks from the park residents as a result.

Most remarks were kind, as when Old Badger said she had never seen such clever squirrels in all her days.

Some remarks were neutral, as when the raven simply commented that toes were neither good nor bad, they just were.

And a few remarks were plainly mean and of course issued forth from the mouths of the weasels, every one of whom remarked that it would probably be a good idea if a certain squirrel mother taught her children some etiquette.

"Etiquette?" repeated Murray when Stumpy told him about this insult. "Isn't that where New Yorkers go for the weekend?"

"No," said Stumpy, "that's *Connecticut*. Etiquette is manners."

"Manners!" shrieked Murray, who enjoyed drama. "Manners! If I had manners, I'd starve!"

(Murray was referring to the fact that he regularly pilfered egg rolls from the Dumpster by the Chinese restaurant down the street. And doughnuts from the bakery Dumpster on the other side of the park. And enchiladas from the Taco Craze Dumpster over by the freeway. The list could go on for miles.)

"Well," said Stumpy, "mothers are sensitive."

"And weasels are rats," said Murray. "Rats in weasel clothing."

Stumpy sighed.

"Gwendolyn would understand," she said. "Gwendolyn understands everything."

Murray nodded in agreement.

"It's because she's a hundred and four years old," he said.

"She is not!" cried Stumpy. "She's just wise."

"Gwendolyn is wise and a hundred and four years old," said Murray.

"You are counting all her past lives she told us about," said Stumpy. "In hermit crab time Gwendolyn is just, well, she is just . . ."

"A hundred and four," said Murray.

"Oh, for goodness' sake," said Stumpy.

Gwendolyn was Stumpy and Murray's dear, dear friend. They could not imagine how they had ever managed without her. Gwendolyn might be a hermit crab, but she understood each of them perfectly. She gave Stumpy—who was something of a worrier—the very best advice about rearing young children. (Gwendolyn's advice always solved the problem.) And Gwendolyn praised Murray's heart, which was actually quite a big heart, but one that Murray hid behind a million funny lines.

Gwendolyn never let her bat friend get away with this.

"You are a shining emblem of love to those children," Gwendolyn often said to Murray.

"A shining plum?" said Murray.

"A shining emblem," said Gwendolyn.

"A shiny Indian?" said Murray.

"Emblem," said Gwendolyn.

"Envelope?" said Murray.

"Oh, for goodness' sake," said Gwendolyn.

But Murray really did hear her. And it made him proud.

The true hero among them all, of course, was the one who said very little about love or courage or wisdom but excelled at all three. And this true hero's name was Kona.

5

Kona was a chocolate Labrador who lived a quiet dog's life with Gwendolyn and their human, Professor Albert.

It had been well over a year since Kona had faced the greatest challenge of his life by rescuing Stumpy's three children. This had happened during a most terrifying ice storm that ravaged the trees of Gooseberry Park, among those the great pin oak where Stumpy's babies had just been born.

With Murray's help, and Gwendolyn's help, Kona managed to hide the children he had rescued by placing them in the Christmas decorations in Professor Albert's basement until Stumpy—who had gone missing in the storm—was found.

It was during this time that Murray developed a strong attachment to television and Oreo cookies. Both were still central to his life. And he had since then sneaked into Professor Albert's house on warm summer days—easing open the screen door with his sneaky little foot—so he

could have a cookie and watch *Jeopardy!* with Gwendolyn. Professor Albert was usually napping in the hammock.

So life for these fine friends and for Professor Albert had been very rich since the ice storm, and the three squirrel babies—once sheltered by a chocolate Labrador and a hermit crab in a human's house—had grown taller and rounder and stronger. And they could hang by their toes.

Life had been very rich and very quiet.

But the very quiet part was about to change.

2

Rain Matters

Gooseberry Park was mystical. That was how Gwendolyn described it once, when Kona took her for a visit to the new home Stumpy and her three children shared with Murray (a very nice sugar maple tree on the south side).

Mystical. A place of enchantment. Gwendolyn was a very spiritual hermit crab, and just as she could recognize a beautiful heart in a person (such as Professor Albert, who this day was helping his third cousin paint a porch), or a beautiful heart in a bat or a squirrel or a dog, she could also recognize it in a place.

There was a stillness to Gooseberry Park that is rare in this world. It seemed that every tree, every flower and bird and creature, had taken a deep breath and settled in. This feeling nearly brought tears to Gwendolyn's eyes as Kona carried her

through the winding paths and alongside the flowing water of Gooseberry Creek.

"How precious, this green place," Gwendolyn whispered.

She and Kona had a lovely visit that day with Stumpy, Murray, Top, Bottom, and Sparrow. It is not often one sees a Labrador, a hermit crab, four squirrels, and a bat sharing egg rolls and powdered doughnuts. But feeding good friends was Murray's second-favorite hobby. (His first favorite was feeding himself.)

It had been a very special afternoon for Gwendolyn and her

friends. It seemed, that early-spring day, that nothing would ever go wrong in Gooseberry Park.

But slowly, and relentlessly, something *was* going wrong. And it involved rain. The friends did not yet know. Even Gwendolyn, who seemed to know many things before they happened, did not know.

A drought was coming.

The green trees, the purple irises, the soft mosses, the tall grasses: Every living thing in Gooseberry Park depended upon rain. Rain created life. And because the rain always came, year after year, the animals did not even think about it. They did not watch for it. They did not wait for it. It always came, just as the night always turned into day. Rain was dependable and constant.

Constancy. Being able to count on something or someone. This is what brings joy, and certainly Kona and Gwendolyn knew this joy. They had lived with dear Professor Albert in his comfortable home for many years.

Gwendolyn had arrived there first. During her long life, Gwendolyn had lived many lives in many places, and her children were scattered far and wide around the world (one even lived in a bunker in Antarctica with a famous scientist). Then one day Gwendolyn found herself in a pet shop. And Professor Albert found her and took her home.

After a time Professor Albert decided he needed a dog. A dog would get him out of the house. Professor Albert was retired and could spend a whole day sitting in his chair with a thick book about elephants or penguins or the planet Mars, and he wouldn't have walked even to the mailbox. Gwendolyn was a perfect pet, but he could not exactly leash her up and take her for a walk in the park. And Gooseberry Park was where Professor Albert knew he should be going every day. It felt so good being there. But he did not want to go alone.

So Professor Albert went to get a chocolate

Labrador puppy from a nice woman on Paradise Lane who had a whole yard full of chocolate puppies, big ones and little ones. And when one little puppy got into Professor Albert's lap and would not leave, it was love at first sight.

That puppy was Kona. And while Professor Albert was very responsible about feeding Kona and teaching him good manners, it was Gwendolyn who really taught Kona about life. In the quiet, dark hours of the night Gwendolyn told

Kona everything that mattered. And one thing that really mattered, Kona learned as he grew into a dog, was constancy.

This summer for the residents of Gooseberry Park, for Kona, for Gwendolyn, and for Professor Albert, rain would no longer be something constant in their lives.

3

Kona's Conviction

O oh, looky," said Murray. "Gummies."

"You promised, Murray," said Stumpy, turning on the faucet in Professor Albert's kitchen.

"Promised what?" Murray asked, doing a little tap dance in the cupboard.

"You promised to take only one treat," said Stumpy.

"I don't think so," said Murray, tappy-tapping on top of a cellophane bag.

"You did," said Stumpy.

"I must have been sleepwalking," said Murray.

"You were not sleepwalking," said Stumpy. "You were flying. You were flying *here*. Right over my head. And you promised. Only one treat. And that was an Oreo, which you have already gobbled."

"Oh, I meant only one treat at a time!" said Murray. "And I never gobble. I nibble. Gobbling is for rats. Rats gobble. And then they burp."

There followed several seconds of loud crinkling that sounded distinctly like a cellophane bag of gummy candies being opened.

"What are you doing, Murray?" asked Stumpy as she carefully put the lid back on the paper cup she'd found outside the Java Love Cafe.

"Mmp. Mmp. Mmp," said Murray.

16

"What?" asked Stumpy.

"Dusting!" said Murray.

Stumpy turned around to look at Murray. He was hugging the cellophane bag to his chest, and he had a red sticky thing between his toes.

"You have a gummy between your toes," said Stumpy.

"Want it?" he asked.

"Definitely not," said Stumpy.

"Good!" said Murray. He popped the red gummy candy into his mouth.

"Mmp," he said.

"Professor Albert is going to worry about his brain again when he sees that open bag," said Stumpy.

"Oh, I can fix *that*!" said Murray.

He stuffed the rest of the candies into his mouth.

"MMP-MMP!" he said, dramatically flinging open his wings.

He swallowed down the lot and threw the bag behind the cupboard.

"That was 'ta-da!'" said Murray. "I said 'ta-da.'"

Stumpy smiled. Murray always made her smile. Even when he was a thief. And a litterer.

"I have the cup of water ready," Stumpy said. "Are you sure you can carry it?"

"Just slide that paper thingy back on it," said Murray.

"You mean the sleeve?" asked Stumpy.

"Right. Put the sleeve on it," said Murray. "After that you can put another sleeve on it. And a hat! And shoes! Then we can name it!"

"I'll just put the sleeve on it," said Stumpy.

"Right," said Murray. "Then I'll grab it with me toesies."

"Thank you, Murray," said Stumpy.

She suddenly looked very serious.

"I am so worried about the water problem," she said.

"Me, too," said Murray. "I haven't soaked in a tub for weeks."

"You don't have a tub, Murray," said Stumpy.

"Exactly," said Murray.

"I think something will have to be done," Stumpy said. "There's been no rain for so long."

"Five months," said Murray, hopping on top of Professor Albert's refrigerator. "Five months and seven days with no moisture and an average high of ninety-one degrees, with nighttime lows in the mid-eighties."

"Murray, have you been sneaking over here to watch the six o'clock news?" Stumpy asked.

"How did you know?" said Murray.

"Because you sound just like Stan the Weatherman," said Stumpy.

"Stan is the Man," said Murray.

They went to join their friends in Professor Albert's living room. (Professor Albert was at his bassoon class.) Gwendolyn's bowl sat in front of the picture window. Outside, the tall dogwood tree in Professor Albert's yard had turned completely brown, its dry leaves dropping with each whisper of wind. But the birdbath was full

of fresh water. Professor Albert filled it four times a day now since the drought. Two jays were showering.

"Did you get your cup of water?" Kona asked Stumpy.

Stumpy nodded.

"Kona," she said, "in the park animals ask day after day whether anyone smells rain coming, whether the eagles see rain coming, and the answer is always no."

"Stan the Man says no, too," added Murray.

"Some of the animals are starting to feel a little desperate," said Stumpy. "Even my children—who usually think only of the next race up the tallest tree—are worried. They told me to be very careful bringing the water home. They asked Murray to hold the cup tight."

"Which I will," said Murray with a firm nod of his head.

Gwendolyn's antennae extended higher, as they always did when she was listening with concern.

"The babies," said Gwendolyn. "Newborns in the park will not thrive."

Stumpy nodded.

"The older animals, too," said Gwendolyn, "are in danger. They cannot travel as far as the others to get a drink of water."

Kona looked at Gwendolyn's antennae, and he knew that the situation had become very serious. For so long they had expected rain just any day. Surely any day.

But newborns and the elderly could not wait for any day. Rain was not here *today*, and they could not survive just by imagining it.

Gwendolyn looked at Kona.

"We must give them help," she said.

Kona sighed. For a moment he wished he were someone else. Maybe one of those dogs on a surfboard in Hawaii.

Then he shook himself out, lifted his head high, remembered who he was, and answered with conviction:

"We will, Gwendolyn. We will."

"Want a gummy?" said Murray, pulling something from his toes.

"Another one?" asked Stumpy.

"I have many little toesies!" said Murray.

4

A Genius

The thermometer in Sammy's Split-Second Lube was registering one hundred degrees when Professor Albert dropped off his car for an oil change the next day. It was too steamy to stay in the garage, so he walked across the street to the dollar discount store.

He browsed among the kitchen gadgets and the potted plants and the bathroom towels. Then he walked down the pet aisle.

And that is when he saw it.

It was a fabulous glass bowl with a beautiful palm tree and a little blue pool *just* the right size for a hermit crab. Gwendolyn would love it!

Professor Albert bought the bowl and a new chew bone for Kona, and he picked up his lubricated car and drove home.

Kona was very happy to get a new bone, and while he worked on that, Professor Albert helped Gwendolyn arrange herself in her new home.

Gwendolyn had always enjoyed the tropics, so she was delighted with the palm tree. And a pool! Gwendolyn dipped a delicate claw in the cool, clear water. Wonderful.

It made Professor Albert very happy to be good to his pets. And he did not even know that he was also good to a bat and four squirrels. But he was. And they tried to be good to him, too.

Stumpy polished Professor Albert's mirrors with a paper towel while she was visiting his house. And she took away the dust bunnies from beneath his couch. When her children came along, she instructed them to weed Professor Albert's flower beds, which they were good at and often tried to do upside down.

And although Murray ate a lot of Professor Albert's snacks, Murray also *brought* him snacks. A fortune cookie from Norm's Chinese Diner. A packet of hot sauce from Taco Craze. The little cups of creamer that people left on the tables outside Java Love. And at Easter, Murray had even tried to bring Professor Albert a whole bag of jelly beans, but Murray couldn't help himself and he had eaten them all before he landed.

So there was great goodwill all around, and it was this feeling that every creature mattered that inspired Kona and Gwendolyn to make a brilliant plan to help the thirsty animals in Gooseberry Park.

First, they decided, they would need a crow.

Kona and Gwendolyn had been staying up late, trying to work out a master plan, and it did not take them long to realize they needed a crow. And not just any crow. They needed Herman.

All crows are smart, but Herman was a *genius*. This was common knowledge in Gooseberry Park. The annual crow chess match actually had to be canceled because Herman had won seven years in a row and everyone was too humiliated to try to beat him after that. Crows have their pride.

Kona and Gwendolyn needed a genius. The problem of getting water to all the newborns and the elderly in Gooseberry Park was a *mathematical* problem, said Gwendolyn. It involved volume and capacity and distribution and a flowchart.

"What's a flowchart?" asked Kona.

"It is a mathematical map," said Gwendolyn.

Kona was terrible at math. Especially fractions. When he and Professor Albert went to Bay Hay and Feed and Professor Albert ordered a quarter pound of oat biscuits, it just did not make sense to Kona. He watched the clerk put the biscuits on the scale, and all the numbers made his head spin. Kona could not understand why oat biscuits had to be so complicated. Couldn't they

just ask for five? It was easy to count to five. But no, the clerk had to put biscuits on the scale, then take biscuits off the scale, then put biscuits back on the scale. Just so Kona could have a snack. A one-quarter-pound snack. Whatever that was.

Kona couldn't wait to find Herman.

Herman lived with his mother and four sisters in a Douglas fir on the east side of the park. They had always been a close family, and Herman would probably never leave home. Herman was something of a misfit out in the world. When all the other crows got raucous and felt like dive-bombing a boy on Rollerblades to make him drop his french fries, Herman held back. He was not raucous. He was quiet. He liked to read and to think. Reading and thinking bores most crows, so they found Herman boring.

But his family didn't. They were all readers and thinkers. At suppertime every member of Herman's family ate with a book in one foot. They hardly said a word at all during supper. Yet

29

they felt quite warm toward one another. And they all felt loved for who they were.

So Kona knew that he would probably find Herman at home.

"Herman!" Kona called up the tree. "Herman! Are you home?"

Kona waited. He waited and waited. He waited and waited and waited.

"Herman?" Kona called again. "Are you there?"

Kona felt that Herman was there. But Herman would not answer him.

"It's just that I have this mathematical problem to solve," called Kona, "and I'm terrible at math and especially fractions, and I was just thinking maybe you—"

Suddenly a shiny black head appeared from between the tall upper branches.

"What kind of problem?" called Herman.

Kona smiled.

"Mathematical," he said. "And moral. It's a moral problem, too."

"Mathematical and moral sounds nuclear," said Herman.

"Oh, no," said Kona. "Nothing like that. Heavens no. This concerns babies and the elderly."

"Precisely," said Herman.

"And the *drought*," said Kona, finally getting to his point.

"Oh," said Herman. "That. What a mess. It's all the fossil fuels, you know."

Kona was starting to feel very dumb. Much like all the crows who used to lose the chess matches.

"I didn't know," said Kona. "But Gwendolyn and I were wondering—"

"Who is Gwendolyn?" asked Herman, hopping to a lower branch. Above him, four crows' heads had popped out and were watching.

"Are those your sisters?" Kona asked.

"Yes. Who is Gwendolyn?" asked Herman, hopping down a few more branches.

"She's my friend, a hermit crab," said Kona. "We live together."

31

Herman cocked his head to one side.

"Hermit crabs fascinate me," he said.

"Me, too," said Kona.

Herman hopped onto a branch that was even with Kona's big chocolate-brown head.

"I am good at solving problems," said Herman.

"I know," said Kona.

And that was the beginning of an amazing adventure.

5

Up All Night

Stumpy was a collector, and most everyone in Gooseberry Park knew that if you wanted to see something interesting, stop by Stumpy's house.

Stumpy rotated her collections, so old ones were always going out and new ones were always coming in.

Murray was in charge of the going out. Everything went to the charity drop box in the Big Bear parking lot. One time, when Stumpy decided to

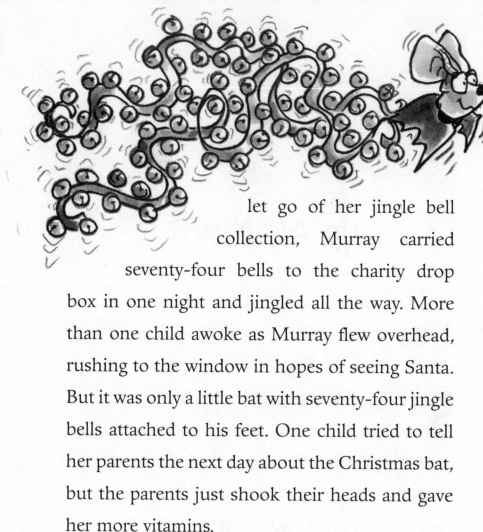

let go of her jingle bell collection, Murray carried seventy-four bells to the charity drop box in one night and jingled all the way. More than one child awoke as Murray flew overhead, rushing to the window in hopes of seeing Santa. But it was only a little bat with seventy-four jingle bells attached to his feet. One child tried to tell her parents the next day about the Christmas bat, but the parents just shook their heads and gave her more vitamins.

So Stumpy's collections were well known, and while the animals of Gooseberry Park very much enjoyed the restaurant napkin tour, the rubber bouncy ball tour, the sparkly bracelet tour, and many others, no one ever imagined that one of Stumpy's collections would turn out to be important. Even lifesaving.

But indeed that was about to happen.

Kona and Gwendolyn and Herman had put their heads together through the dark hours of the night, and they had made a plan. A plan, said Herman, for the dog days.

Herman explained that dog days were long, hot summer days. He said that humans call them dog days because that's when dogs just lie about and sleep all day, but that really it has to do with the dog constellation Canis Major in the summer sky.

"Well," Kona said, feeling rather offended, "not all dogs sleep all day."

"Indeed," said Herman. "It's just the law of averages."

"The what?" asked Kona.

"Some dogs do and some dogs don't, dear," said Gwendolyn.

"Exactly," said Kona.

Certainly Kona was no dog-day dog. In fact, he'd

hardly had any
sleep at all what
with staying up
all night with
Gwendolyn and
Herman working
on the plan, and
looking after
Professor Albert all day.
Why, he had been so groggy
that Professor Albert even noticed and gave him
extra peanut butter crunchies, which did, actually,
perk Kona right up.

But they had made a Master Plan—Kona,
Gwendolyn, and Herman—and Herman had
drawn it all on the back of a VOTE FOR JEFF sign
he'd found beside the library book depository
(which was where he and his family borrowed
their books). It was, said Gwendolyn, inspired.

And one very important word of that Master
Plan was "straws."

Well, everyone knew who had a lot of *those*. An entire collection, in fact!

The Master Plan also contained other vital parts. They were:

a cat

a possum

a raccoon

200 owls

20 packs of chewing gum

"It should work," said Herman.

Kona and Gwendolyn very much hoped so. But they were a little worried about the owl part. Because owls just hate teamwork. Which is why they never play catch, like crows. So getting two hundred owls to do the same thing on the same night in the same way for the same reason . . .

It would take a pretty good talker. It would take somebody who knew how to work a crowd. It would take . . . *a motivational speaker*.

Luckily, somebody's long-lost brother was about to show up. Somebody's long-lost brother

who was a motivational speaker and who just happened to be between jobs. Meaning, out of work. And sort of mooching off family. Mooching as in hanging around and eating all their stuff while he was waiting to get motivated himself.

Company was about to come knocking on Murray's door.

6

Morton

He is eating me out of house and home!" cried Murray as he opened up Stumpy's cupboards. "And he's been here only three hours!"

Murray peered inside a Roy Rogers sippy cup.

"Don't you eat anything besides nuts?" Murray said.

"I love nuts," said Stumpy.

"I'm *going* nuts!" wailed Murray.

He looked inside a little red pencil box Stumpy had found by the children's picnic tables.

"Ooh!" he said. "Raisins. I love raisins."

Murray stuffed a footful of raisins into his mouth.

He swallowed.

"'If you can dream it, you can do it!'" Murray said.

"Do what?" asked Stumpy.

"I don't know!" cried Murray. "Ask my crazy brother! He says it all the time!"

"Murray," said Stumpy. "It's been only three hours. Three hours is not 'all the time.'"

"Time," said Murray. "Do you know what Morton says about time?"

"What?" asked Stumpy.

"He says time is an *illusion*," said Murray. "I don't even know what 'illusion' means. I think maybe it has something to do with those health-food cookies."

"'Illusion' means something that seems to be real but is not real," said Stumpy.

"I was close," said Murray. "Anyway, I can tell you that three hours with my long-lost brother is *really* making me lose my mind! Not to mention that I'm eating all your raisins."

"Surely he's not that bad," said Stumpy. "And he's supposed to say things that motivate. That's his job."

"He sure does motivate me," said Murray. "He is motivating me to move to Florida."

Suddenly there was a knock at Stumpy's door.

"Anyone home?" someone called.

"Shhh," said Murray.

"Yes! Yes, come in, Morton!" said Stumpy. "So nice to meet you!"

Stumpy could see the family resemblance in Murray and Morton. Morton was older and a little balding, but the big brown eyes were just the same.

Stumpy invited Morton to stay for a snack. She put together a nice plate of walnuts and raisins for them all and then asked Morton to tell her a bit about himself.

"Well," said Morton, "my journey began with a single step."

Murray rolled his eyes.

"And as I have always said," Morton continued, "if you can dream it, you—"

"*Can do it!*" finished Murray. "Which is what is happening right now. I am *dreaming* I can leave and I am *doing* it!"

Murray flew out the door.

"See you later!" he called.

Stumpy smiled at Morton.

"You were saying?" she said, passing him the plate of food.

Morton smiled and reached for another raisin.

"It all began at a Zen retreat in Half Moon Bay," Morton began. "I was searching for answers, and in time I discovered that the answers were already within me."

"Oh, I know just what you mean," said Stumpy.

"Gwendolyn calls it divine wisdom. She has a lot of it."

"And who is Gwendolyn?" asked Morton, as had so many others before him. It seemed that all roads led to Gwendolyn.

"Well, I'll tell you—" said Stumpy.

"First," Morton interrupted, "have you any blueberries? Or maybe melon? Apples? If the answer is no, then that is perfectly fine. We must be at peace with what is. But if there is any fruit at hand, that would be stellar."

"No," said Stumpy, shaking her head. "So sorry. Just nuts. And raisins. I found the raisins in a pencil box a little boy left in the park. The blueberries, raspberries—everything we love to eat in summer—are not here this year. It is the drought, you know."

Suddenly Stumpy felt very sad. She felt quite close to tears.

"Oh my," said Morton. "I am an oaf."

"Oh, no," said Stumpy. "Not at all. You've only

just flown in. You could not know how it has
been."

Something in Stumpy's face was so honest and
so heartfelt that Morton could not help asking:

"And how has it been?"

Stumpy took a deep breath.

Then she said, "I will
tell you what drought
is. Drought is
worry. It is
worry

above all else. And we mothers, we worry most of all. The streams dry up, and then the creeks, and then even parts of the river. Do you know how many soda cans are at the bottom of the river? I didn't, until the water dried up.

"The plants die. And everyone who can travel begins to leave. I can't tell you how many hummingbirds I know who've flown to Canada. So many good-byes.

"And there's so much dust. It affects the children. The baby chipmunks cough as often as the little girls and boys who sit beneath the shade trees with their mothers. The ground is all dust, the wind blows, and babies cough.

"And mothers worry about food. Even nuts can rot in the heat. But those whose children depend on berries and juicy green leaves and those perfect, round little crab apples that always grew in the orchards on the north side . . . They are afraid the food will be gone. It is not yet all gone. But they worry."

Morton nodded sympathetically. Morton had always been a good listener.

"But thirst, Morton, that is the immediate threat," continued Stumpy. "Thirst. Gooseberry Creek has dried up, and we have so many new babies in the park who are quite fragile. We also have the elderly—the ancient skunks and gophers who move so slowly, and the older pigeons who can hardly fly at all. They, too, are quite fragile.

"Drought is worry, Morton," said Stumpy. "Even for Murray. I have seen him sneak away with cups of ice he found on cafe tables and bring them to my children to make sure they are all right."

Stumpy paused. Then she began to lighten.

"But now, Morton, there has come a new ray of hope," she said.

"Gwendolyn?" Morton asked instinctively.

Stumpy smiled.

"Gwendolyn is part of the hope. But there are also others. Others who are making a plan to help."

"And how may I help?" Morton asked.

And although he did not yet know it, in that moment Morton became a volunteer. A volunteer motivational speaker.

They were all certainly going to need one.

7

Only One Owl

Kona was elected to be goodwill ambassador to the owl population in Gooseberry Park. Gwendolyn and Herman and Kona had all cast votes, and the result was Kona 2 and Herman 1. (Kona had voted for Herman because Kona liked him, and also because—unlike Kona—Herman would not have to stand at the bottom of a tree hoping an owl would talk to him.)

It was a job fraught with risk. Owls are not only uninterested in teamwork. They are also uninterested in anything having to do with humans.

Kona could not, of course, imagine being uninterested in humans. Why, Professor Albert was practically his hero. Kona had watched Professor Albert do amazing things, like risking his life to rescue a rabbit on the freeway and wading into the river to untangle a turtle caught in fishing twine. Professor Albert could build birdhouses and rewire old radios, and when he set up his train set in the basement one Christmas, Kona was positively mesmerized. Kona knew many wonderful creatures with wonderful talents, but none of them could create a tiny town with tiny trees and people and dogs and houses and then make a train race around all of them with its whistle blowing.

How could owls be uninterested in humans? But, according to Herman, they were. Maybe it had something to do with being nocturnal. Owls were not usually awake when humans were doing things that might impress them.

But the Master Plan required that two hundred owls be willing not only to work as a team, but also to fly themselves straight into the world of humans.

And two out of the three master planners were convinced that Kona could talk the owls into it.

"How do I talk to two hundred owls?" Kona asked Herman. "How do I even find two hundred owls?"

"You need find only one," said Herman. "Her name is Augustina. Convince Augustina, and the other one hundred ninety-nine will fall in line. I'll take you to her tonight."

"I hope she doesn't peck me on the head," said Kona.

"Oh, no," said Herman. "Only jays do that."

"Yes, jays for sure," said Kona. "I wish they would just politely ask me to go away."

"She could, however, bite you on the nose," said Herman. "Be careful of your nose."

Kona thought about his nose. Then he thought about a surfboard in Hawaii.

Kona sighed.

"All right, Herman," he said. "See you at midnight."

Kona hoped Augustina would be in a friendly mood toward noses.

8

The Master Plan

A Master Plan always looks very important on paper, and the Master Plan for Gooseberry Park was no exception. Herman had suggested they show it to Augustina, so when he and Kona started out for the park at midnight (Gwendolyn unlocked the door, as she always did when friends would come and go), the Master Plan had been neatly folded by Herman and tucked under Kona's collar.

It was a very bold plan and would require all participants to be very daring. Herman had drawn it all out quite carefully, in flowchart fashion.

When Kona first saw the plan on paper, he had to ask Herman what "Houston, we have landed!" meant.

Herman said it was what astronauts always say when their rockets land on the moon. It meant "mission accomplished."

"Who is Houston?"

"Not a who, a what," said Herman.

"What?" asked Kona.

"Yes," said Herman.

"No, what?" asked Kona.

"Yes," said Herman.

"But *what*?" asked Kona.

"Exactly," said Herman.

Kona decided he would just look it up in the encyclopedia.

Kona and Herman enjoyed their walk together

to the park. Herman told Kona about the history of the planet and how an asteroid had brought about the extinction of the dinosaurs. Herman said that scientists think that birds today are relatives of all those extinct dinosaurs.

"Really?" said Kona.

Herman said that it had something to do with the little bones in their wings.

"You mean Murray is a relative of a dinosaur?" asked Kona.

"Not Murray," said Herman. "Murray is a mammal."

"Murray's not a bird like you?" said Kona. "But he flies."

"So do squirrels and they're not birds," said Herman.

"Squirrels fly?" asked Kona.

"Some of them," said Herman.

"Well, don't tell Stumpy's children," said Kona. "They fall on their heads often enough as it is."

Kona was quiet for a few moments.

Then Kona said, "Herman, do you think there will be another asteroid? Do you think we will become extinct?"

Herman seemed to consider the question very carefully.

Finally he said, "I think that there is, for all of us, a greater danger than asteroids."

"What is it?" asked Kona.

"Greed," said Herman. "I think it is greed."

Kona did not understand what Herman meant. But he knew Gwendolyn would understand. He would ask her when he got home. He hoped he would not also have to ask for a Band-Aid for his nose.

They arrived at the park. The park was dark and beautiful. Kona was rarely in Gooseberry Park this late. Once, when Top had a fever and Stumpy needed a thermometer at two in the morning. And there was the time when Murray was worried another ice storm would come and had asked Kona to stand guard in case they had to save the children again. (Ice never came, but Kona did have to walk through two feet of snow to get back home before Professor Albert got up for breakfast.)

The nighttime park was beautiful. And it was also very active. All the night creatures were out: possums, bats, owls, raccoons, mice. And others were trying to get some sleep: squirrels, chipmunks, bluebirds, wrens.

Kona was starting to feel a little nervous. In

the daytime Kona felt that he belonged to the park. Actually, he felt sometimes that the park belonged to him. It is a heady experience to be a chocolate Labrador walking his owner through Gooseberry Park. As Professor Albert once said, "It feels as if we have the world on a string, Kona." If that meant confidence, then Kona had to agree. A dog in a park on a sunny day with his owner is nothing but confident.

But now it was after midnight. And Kona knew he did not belong.

"I hope Augustina likes dogs," Kona said as Herman guided him to her roost.

"Just be yourself," Herman told Kona. "You are enough just as you are."

Hearing that, Kona lifted his head higher. Being enough was so important to him. And Herman had said he was.

Kona was ready to meet Augustina.

Herman flew up into the branches of an enormous walnut tree, and Kona waited.

"Good evening," said a voice suddenly behind him.

Kona almost jumped out of his fur. He turned around, and there before him was a calm and powerful owl who Kona knew could be no one other than Augustina.

Herman flew down from the branches and introduced them.

"It is an honor to meet you," Kona told Augustina. "I didn't hear you coming."

"Few do," said Augustina. Her very large eyes blinked once.

Herman pulled the Master Plan from Kona's collar. He then spread it on the ground so Kona could explain.

"Two hundred of us, you say," Augustina said to Herman.

Herman nodded.

"Describe to me very carefully this brilliant plan," said Augustina.

So Kona described it.

There was only one reliable source of stored water in town. And that one reliable source was the water truck at the fire house.

"It's always full," noted Kona.

If the fire fighters could be tricked to leave the fire house for a while (Kona pointed to POSSUM), and if the fire house door could be unlocked from

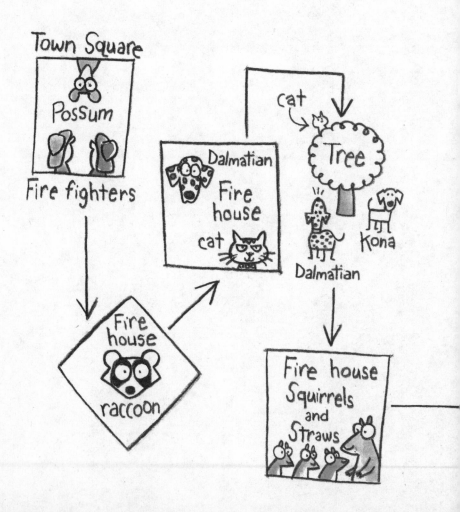

the inside (Kona pointed to RACCOON), then the fire house dog (DALMATION) could also be tricked to leave the fire house for a while (CAT), so that Stumpy could open up the tank on the water truck and she and her children (SQUIRRELS) could fill dozens and dozens of straws with water and seal them up with chewing gum.

Kona stopped for a moment to catch his breath. Augustina blinked while she waited. Kona was nervous because now he was getting to the part about the owls.

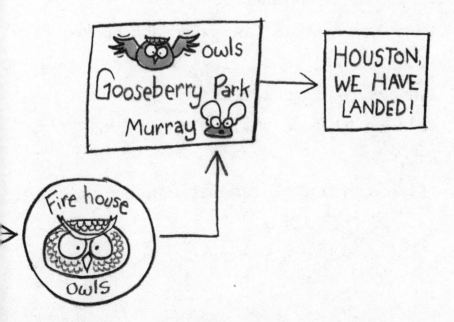

"We need fliers," Kona said. "Silent nighttime fliers with binocular vision."

He pointed to OWLS on the plan as he looked at Augustina with great sincerity. (And there are few things that look so sincere as a Labrador who wants something.)

"If two hundred of you could fly into the fire house," said Kona, "and collect the straws of water and then deliver them to all who need them . . ."

Kona took another deep breath.

"Then we will have done something magnificent together," he finished.

Augustina examined the paper. She blinked several times.

She pointed to a name.

"Murray," she said. "I know Murray. What is his part?"

"Murray's friend Stumpy has a glow-in-the-dark watch," said Kona.

"I have heard," said Augustina.

"And," Kona continued, "when the owls arrive back at the park with the water, Murray will shine the watch on every nest and every burrow where someone is in need. He will know where the need is. Murray knows the park like the back of his foot."

Augustina's head turned slowly to the far, far left and then slowly to the far, far right. Then back to center.

"Many here," she said, "are in crisis."

Kona and Herman nodded.

Augustina was silent. She remained silent, in fact, for several minutes. Owls need time to think.

Kona felt his heart pounding.

Finally she spoke:

"Tell me when to have them ready. And you shall have your two hundred fliers."

If Labradors and crows could cry, surely tears would have flowed.

As it was, Kona and Herman said simply, "Thank you," which is all, really, an owl ever needs to hear.

So now it was onward to find a possum, a raccoon, and a cat who would play their parts.

Kona wasn't worried. In fact, he already had just the cat in mind. And possums and raccoons are always up for tricks.

Suddenly it seemed that Houston was actually going to see them land!

9

Decoys

Kona's friend Conroy the cat agreed to be one of the decoys in the Master Plan. And Stumpy's friend Henrietta the possum agreed to be another. Henrietta had a family of eight who traveled everywhere with her on her back, and she was passionate about helping with the

Master Plan, for she wanted to represent all mothers everywhere. Conroy the cat wanted to help just because he thought his part was funny.

But finding a raccoon to do *his* part of the plan took a bit more trouble. Raccoons keep very strict schedules. If a raccoon sifts through a certain Dumpster at a certain location at eleven every night, that is exactly what he wants to do the very next night: Certain Dumpster. Certain location. Eleven.

So it took some extra legwork to find a raccoon who was not so compulsive that he could not change his routine for a night. But Murray found one. The raccoon's name was Robby, and for the price of seven egg rolls and two boxes of Hot Tamales, he joined the team.

Murray was so stressed from having to give away all his snacks that he had to make a Reiki appointment with Gwendolyn. Gwendolyn said that Reiki was good for stress.

"But you aren't even touching me," said

Murray, lying
on Professor Albert's
coffee table.

"I am reorganizing your
energy," said Gwendolyn.

"Okay, but just make sure I still have all me
toesies when you're done," said Murray.

"I will, dear," said Gwendolyn. She moved her
claws in the air just above Murray's body.

"And how are you feeling now?" Gwendolyn
asked.

Murray didn't answer. He had dropped off to
sleep, a bit of drool drip-dripping from his mouth.

69

"Success," said Gwendolyn with a smile. She covered him with a clean dish towel so he wouldn't catch a chill.

While Murray was napping, with Gwendolyn keeping him company, Kona was giving instructions to three vital members of the team. The big night was tomorrow night, and there were some things to rehearse. According to the flowchart, Henrietta would first play her part. Then Robby would leap into action. Then Conroy would jump in, with Kona as backup.

It was all designed to get the fire fighters and the dalmatian out of the fire house, and the squirrels and the owls in.

So the three decoys needed to rehearse. Kona gathered them all under a picnic shelter in the park.

"Henrietta, your job is to pretend to faint," said Kona.

"Right," said Henrietta as her eight children hung on and stared at the big chocolate Labrador.

Henrietta then pretended to fall into a swoon, rolling over onto her side. The children were still hanging on.

"Excellent," said Kona. "But can you do it while hanging from a traffic light?"

"Positively," said Henrietta.

"And the children—can they hang on?" asked Kona.

Eight little possum heads nodded.

"Fantastic," said Kona. "When people see a possum hanging from the traffic light in the Town Square—which only a very tall ladder can reach—whom do you think they will call for the rescue?"

"Fire fighters," said eight little possums.

Henrietta smiled proudly.

"Right," said Kona.

"Now, Robby," continued Kona, "your job is to sneak into the fire house attic tomorrow night, and as soon as the fire fighters are called to the rescue, you will come out of the attic and unlock the fire house door from the inside."

"Simple," said Robby. "Sneaking into attics is my specialty." Robby popped a Hot Tamale into his mouth.

"Fabulous," said Kona.

Kona turned next to Conroy the cat.

"I know," said Conroy. "You don't even have to tell me. I stroll in and agitate the dog."

"The *dalmatian*," Kona clarified. "You get the dalmatian to chase you out of the fire house and up a tree. Then I'll come join him in the barking. Dalmatians are very high strung. Together you and I can keep that dog barking forever."

"Cool," said Conroy.

"And after that," Kona said to them all, "it's showtime."

10

Nerves

The night before a major undertaking is always a night of anxiousness, and Kona and all of his friends were feeling their share of it.

In front of Professor Albert's picture window, Kona was pacing as Gwendolyn read aloud passages from a book Morton had dropped off. The book's title was *Affirmations for the Faint of Heart,* and it had much good advice for anyone feeling anxious.

"'There is no fear so great that time with a

friend will not soothe,'" read Gwendolyn.

"Oh, that's a good one," said Kona, stopping his pacing for a moment. "I do feel soothed by being with you, Gwendolyn."

"And I do with you," said Gwendolyn. "Let's continue reading."

So that is how Kona and Gwendolyn handled their anxiousness.

In the tree they shared, Stumpy and Murray were dealing with their nerves in their own ways.

Stumpy was rearranging her closets. Tidying always brought a sense of calm to Stumpy. So she dug in and had built quite a big mound of throwaways and another of keepers. It helped tremendously. Everyone was counting on her tomorrow night to open the plug on the tank of the water truck. Stumpy had cracked open probably thousands of black walnuts in her life and could not imagine a water plug tripping her up. But still, she was a little anxious. So she tidied.

Her three children were sleeping like logs. Children are always optimistic, and this unfailingly helps them get a good night's sleep, even with a major undertaking on the calendar.

But Murray, like Stumpy, was also up late. He was wide awake and mentally counting all the nests and burrows in the park that would receive the water deliveries tomorrow night. He tried to count them on his toes. But since he had only ten toes, that didn't last long. So Murray just closed his eyes, and in his mind he flew from nest to nest, burrow to burrow, to make certain he would not miss a single location.

He also ran outside frequently to make sure the lifetime battery in Stumpy's glow-in-the-dark watch was living up to its promise. The watch hung by Stumpy's front door as a porch light, and tonight it glowed as bright as ever.

Then Murray popped a powdered doughnut hole into his mouth and closed his eyes and started counting the babies and the old ones again.

In the guest room, Morton was chewing twenty packs of gum. Morton had been asked by Kona to do two things: chew twenty packs of gum and be on call tomorrow night in case anyone needed motivating. Morton had felt very capable of doing both. So he chewed an incredible amount of gum while he solved a crossword puzzle, and then he turned in for the night.

At Herman's home everyone was sitting up with Herman as a show of moral support. Herman's mother and four sisters did not know any specifics of the Master Plan. But just because you don't know how to play the game does not mean you can't sit on the sidelines and cheer.

Herman was obsessed with timing. With his mathematically inclined Chess Master brain, he had calculated the time everyone would need tomorrow night, down to the second. It was especially important that Stumpy's timing for opening the water tank plug was accurate, and after observing her open a series of black walnuts, Herman had calculated that she would need four seconds to do it.

But the children—Top, Bottom, and Sparrow—

they were the wild cards. Children are always hard to calculate to the second, no matter what they're doing. That is because they are creative and therefore easily distracted. Just when a child seems to be settling in quite nicely with a set of crayons and a coloring book, he can suddenly jump up and start marching around and playing his tooty horn.

So Herman was very careful to teach the three young squirrels to *focus*. He told them he would never have won a single game of chess without it.

Top, Bottom, and Sparrow all admired Herman very much, and they wanted to do their job well for him. So they had practiced focus in Professor Albert's kitchen sink, filling it up with water, dunking in the straws, and plugging them with chewing gum on both ends.

Herman had timed their efforts and calculated that the children could fill up and plug thirty straws per minute. Based on volume, proportion,

and density of all the babies and the elderly in need of water enough to last one more month of drought, Herman's final equation equaled a sum of four hundred straws. In thirteen minutes and twenty seconds three squirrel children should have four hundred straws plugged and ready to go. Herman rounded the time up to thirteen minutes and thirty seconds to allow for distractions.

With two hundred owls carrying a straw in each foot over a distance of 1.7 miles from the fire house to the park, and allowing time for distribution, the entire Master Plan would be accomplished in thirty-three minutes and seventeen seconds.

Herman explained this to his mother and four sisters to recheck accuracy.

They nodded in encouragement and applauded at the end.

Herman went to bed.

The team was ready.

11

If You Can
Dream It . . .

Hello, this is the fire department."

"There's a mother possum! Hanging from a traffic light in the Town Square! And eight possum babies are hanging with her!"

"You say a *possum*, ma'am?"

"Not just any possum! A *mama* possum!"

Silence.

"We don't usually do possums, ma'am."

"Well, she's about twenty feet up, and we've got cars honking and children crying for a fire fighter to come to the rescue. Why did you become a fire fighter, anyway, if you're not going to rescue a possum family twenty feet up?"

Silence.

"Ring the bell, mister! Ring the bell! We've got a crisis here!"

"All right, ma'am. Ringing the bell, ma'am."

The fire house bell rang loud and clear, and all the fire fighters in the fire house jumped on the ladder truck, and away they went.

Henrietta, so far, had done superbly. And her eight children, too.

While the fire fighters were heading for the Town Square, Robby the raccoon was lifting up an attic door inside the fire house, sliding down the fire house pole, and grabbing a biscuit off the dinner table on his way to the front door.

He lifted the latch and Conroy stepped in.

"Where's the dog?" asked Conroy.

"In the office over there." Robby pointed. "He's sleeping."

"Not for long," said Conroy, grinning.

"Good luck!" said Robby on his way out.

Conroy walked across the fire house floor, into the office, and jumped on top of a file cabinet.

"Meow," he said.

Bark, bark, bark, bark, bark, bark, bark, bark, bark, bark, bark, bark, bark, bark, bark!

"Want to play tag?" Conroy asked when the dalmatian stopped barking to take a breath. "I'm It!"

And Conroy leaped over the dog's head and ran toward the open door. In nine seconds (just as Herman had calculated) the dalmatian was out of the fire house and Conroy was up a tree.

"Meow, meow, meow," said Conroy for effect.

Bark, bark, bark, bark, bark, bark, bark!

"Hurry!" said Kona, coming from behind the fire house with Stumpy and her children. "Hurry inside!"

Stumpy and the children ran inside the fire house and hopped onto the tank truck, while Kona went off to contribute to the dalmatian agitation.

Stumpy took a look at the water tank plug. Twist, twist, snap, lift. Four seconds flat.

A box of four hundred straws was strapped to Top with a rubber band. And Bottom had his arms around the big ball of chewing gum Morton had dropped off that morning. Stumpy unstrapped the box, opened it, and put the gum ball into position.

"All right, children," she said. "Go!"

Top, Bottom, and Sparrow set to dunking and plugging. They were amazingly quick. But then Top noticed the shiny fire house pole over in the corner of the room.

"Wow!" he said. "A real fire house pole! I've never seen one in person! Look how shiny! I bet it's so fun. Do you think I could—"

"*Dunk!*" shouted Sparrow. "*Dunk!*"

Top resumed dunking after the ten-second distraction that had been calculated into Herman's flowchart.

But as the children dunked and plugged, and Stumpy stood by, ready to hand the full straws to the owls when they arrived, a bit of a problem was brewing back in the park.

There, 199 owls had shown up to be fliers, just as Augustina had promised. But the two hundredth owl was missing, and that was Augustina herself. She had sprained a wing and was on bed rest for a week.

And no Augustina meant no teamwork. A group of owls is called a parliament for good reason: They rely on a leader to give them direction. Without a leader they tended to argue. Even brawl. A parliament in a brawl is

87

a disaster. Nothing gets done, and everybody ends up looking scruffy.

So in Gooseberry Park, 199 owls were huffing and puffing about the right way to organize the flying—in a straight line or in ranks of seven or in pairs of two or in a pyramid style. And the seconds that Herman had so carefully calculated were ticking away, because naturally every owl had his opinion and he voiced it quite rudely, and a few owls even started to shove and push a bit. And when all this occurred, just as Kona had anticipated it might, the worst possible result happened:

The owls became *de*motivated.

So while the squirrels in the fire house dunked and plugged with all their might, and Conroy meowed, and Henrietta swung upside down in the Town Square, 199 owls started to question whether this was all really necessary, and why should they work for a crow and a dog anyway, and what if they became trapped inside the fire house, and would it not be easier to go back home and just *wait* for the drought to be over? Because after all, nothing in life is permanent, and that includes droughts, and why not just approach the whole problem by way of the *mind*, rather than the body, and just *visualize* rain coming? That should work. Just *visualize* the water problem going away, and surely the power of the mind would show itself to be superior to flying 1.7 miles out and back in pairs. Or ranks of seven. Or in a pyramid style. Or a straight line.

Better just to call it a night and go home.

"*Wait!*" called a strong voice from high in a tree. "Wait!"

The owls all looked up. And there was Morton, wings spread wide, a kind of glow all around him (it was Stumpy's watch, which Murray had loaned him for some drama).

Morton began to speak. He had thirty-five seconds, so he knew he'd better make it good.

"There is in each one of you," Morton began, "a hero. And this is your moment of reckoning. Your moment of reckoning! Will you listen to the voice within you that wants you to fail? Or will you be better than that? Will you fly to the heights of greatness you never imagined? *This* is your moment of reckoning!"

Morton pulled out every motivational line he'd ever used on a crowd. Group hypnosis was really what it was all about, and Morton was a master. He spoke passionately, intensely, meaningfully for thirty-two seconds, and then he finished with the zinger that always worked at the end:

"If you can dream it . . . you can do it."

And 199 owls, eyes shining with a new glow of self-awareness, pulled themselves together into one long, straight line, and off they flew.

Morton dropped the watch back to Murray, and then he caught up with the parliament.

The owls were short one set of toes. And Morton could carry two straws as well as Augustina could have done.

And besides, Morton thought, maybe this was his moment of reckoning, too.

12

. . . You Can Do It

There is perhaps nothing so sweet in this life as to be in need, to hope for help, and to have help arrive. And so it was that remarkable night in Gooseberry Park.

Most creatures—in fact, perhaps all creatures—are brave. They try to meet life's challenges with courage and with action. The earth's forests and prairies and mountains and seas are filled with greatness. Animals ask almost nothing of life except that it give them a chance—a chance to be their best.

So it had been a terrible blow to the animals in Gooseberry Park to be rendered nearly helpless in the face of forces beyond their control. They could not control the movement of the rains. They could not control the heat of the sun. They could not control all the new machines that had created so many poisons for which the good green Earth was unprepared.

The animals did their best. They adapted. They conserved their energies, they learned to eat different things, they had fewer babies.

But water: Water was vital, and without it they would die. And who among them had ever imagined that right there in Gooseberry Park— where humans strolled with their infants and had picnics and threw Frisbees—there would be so great a risk to the lives of many of the park's creatures, namely the very young and the very old.

Fortunately, many creatures have not only great courage but great heart as well. And this night those hearts were beating strong.

At precisely 10:40 p.m., 199 owls plus one volunteer motivational speaker left Gooseberry Park on a mission of mercy.

The owls flew silently. With binocular vision they could see the fire fighters attempting to wake up Henrietta (as her eight babies ate granola bars someone had thought to bring). The owls could see a yellow tabby cat in a tree with a dalmatian barking vigorously beneath it, a chocolate Labrador cheering him on. The owls could see the fire house door, wide open, and the four squirrels inside with four hundred straws filled with precious water for pickup.

Then, capably and swiftly, the owls flew through that open door with precision and grasped a straw in each foot, and, capably and swiftly, they flew away.

Morton, lagging behind because the owls were such strong fliers, straggled in for the last two straws.

"Morton!" cried the squirrels in unison.

Morton gave a big grin, and at that moment he looked exactly like his younger brother, Murray.

"I stopped talking the talk and decided to walk the walk!" he said, grabbing the final straws.

Away he flew.

"What did he mean, Mama?" Sparrow asked her mother.

Stumpy smiled.

"He meant that love is not just what you say," she answered. "It's what you do."

Stumpy looked at the beautiful faces of the three young squirrels.

"And tonight, my good children, you loved."

13

Perfectly

Murray had a reputation for bumping into things. His bat radar had always been a little deficient. But whenever he borrowed Stumpy's glow-in-the-dark watch, Murray was a brilliant navigator.

So this night, when the two hundred fliers arrived back in the park, Murray was at the top of his game. Flying with the glowing watch hanging around his neck, Murray led the owls to each and every nest and burrow in the park that waited for

a delivery. Mouse mothers stood in their door-
ways watching for him. Old chipmunks sat up
past their bedtimes. Help was on the way, and no
one would be thirsty anymore.

During the unfolding of the Master Plan this
important night, two members of the planning
team had been engaged only in spirit.

In her glass bowl, with its exotic palm tree and
sparkling blue pool of water, Gwendolyn had
watched the evening sky as she meditated on

all things succeeding and had asked the good spirits of the universe to help her friends this night.

And Herman—his job as the behind-the-scenes mathematical genius now completed—was in his home reading *The Incredible Journey*, the book in one foot and a stopwatch in the other. His mother and his four sisters were reading books, too. And when, every few minutes, Herman would click the watch off and say something like "The cat is in" or "The tank is open" and then click the watch on again, his family would stop reading and smile approvingly.

Thirty-three minutes and seventeen seconds. Herman had never lived so intense a time in his life as when he counted down the minutes and seconds while the Master Plan unfolded that night, experiencing every moment with his imagination, becoming every character in every scene, scanning every detail and every movement until, as Herman dreamed it could be, the very last delivery was made to the very last address.

It was a challenge to concentrate on both *The Incredible Journey* and the countdown of the Master Plan, but Herman did it anyway because he had always been good at thinking about two things at once, and also because he thought the stress would give him a terrible stomachache if he didn't.

Herman read. He counted. He waited. Until, at 11:18 p.m., someone softly called out from below. It was the call for which Herman had been waiting.

And just as had happened in a time that now seemed so long ago, Herman's shiny black head appeared from between the tall upper branches.

"Herman?" called Kona from below.

"Did we solve the problem?" asked Herman.

"Perfectly," said Kona.

Perfectly

There was a moment of silence.

"I'm going to bed now," said Herman.

"Me, too. Good night, Herman," said Kona.

"Good night."

14

Home

Rain had now been falling for nine days in a row. Professor Albert had every window in the house open so he could smell it. The drops splashed through the window screens onto Kona's brown nose and into Gwendolyn's sparkling blue pool.

Everything had started growing again. Bright green needles were sprouting on the pines, and even the hydrangea bushes—which everyone had thought were long gone—had lifted up and produced tight, round, tiny balls of pink and blue flowers. Earthworms pushed up through the wet brown soil of all the yards and gardens, and even hummingbirds were sipping from the salvia again. Spiders wove strands of silk glistening wet with chains of pearls. Basements even flooded a bit; but fortunately for Kona and his friends, the basement in Professor Albert's house stayed nice and dry, all the Christmas decorations still safe, and Murray's stash of cheese curls tucked into the angel tree topper still crispy.

When Stan the Weatherman had finally predicted rain, almost a month had passed since the Night of the Owls (as everyone now liked to call it), and Kona and Herman and Gwendolyn had started worrying they might need a Master Plan Part Two. But they didn't after all.

Still, the drought was sure to be remembered by everyone for a long time. Already flower beds in the Town Square that had not survived the heat had been replaced by little cacti and succulents, which needed hardly any water.

"Those are called 'hens and chicks,'" Stumpy explained to Murray as they explored the square one evening to see the changes.

"Ohh, I see them!" said Murray. He pointed to a large, round succulent in what used to be the petunia bed.

"There's the hen," he said.

Stumpy nodded.

"And all those little ones are the chicks," said Murray.

Stumpy nodded again.

"I think we should name them," Murray said.

"Murray, you want to name everything," said Stumpy.

"Let's call the hen Fluffy," said Murray.

"Oh, for goodness' sake," said Stumpy.

Flower beds were, of course, not the only things that changed when the drought finally ended. Many people up and moved away, and so did many animals. It had all been too much. A lot of them headed for the rain forest in Olympic National Park.

But not Professor Albert. Not Kona and Gwendolyn. Not Stumpy and Murray and Top and Bottom and Sparrow. Not Herman.

This was their home. They loved it here. They couldn't imagine being anywhere else or with anyone else. They wanted to stay.

And Morton.

Morton had been a wanderer for almost all of his life, and he had never known what it is to remain in place and watch the seasons come and go year after year, to watch children grow up, to watch old houses weather and fade, to watch saplings grow into maple trees.

Morton had been Murray's long-lost brother in more ways than one. Because Morton had actually, at times, *felt* lost. As if he did not know where he belonged. And belonging is so important for anyone. If someone ever asked Gwendolyn what the grayest time of her life was, she always said it was the two months she spent in a bowl in the pet shop. This was because, she said, she belonged to no one. Gwendolyn said that it was a good experience, though, because ever after, she understood everyone who felt lost, and she could promise that one day, if they were patient and trusting in Life, they would find where they belonged.

And so the drought, and all of the hardship and worry it had brought to everyone in Gooseberry Park, turned out to have what is called a silver lining for a certain long-lost brother who had grown weary of fancy thoughts and fancy language about how to achieve a successful life.

What Morton really wanted, he discovered, was someone nice to eat dinner with every day. So he found a little birch tree near Stumpy and Murray's sugar maple.

And he unpacked his Zen cookbook.

And he stayed.